For Anna

Kane/Miller Book Publishers, Inc.
First American Edition 2009
by Kane/Miller Book Publishers, Inc.
La Jolla, California

First published in Germany by Ravensburger Buchverlag in 2008

Copyright © Ravensburger Buchverlag

Kane Miller, A Division of EDC Publishing
P.O. Box 470663
Tulsa, OK 74147-0663
www.kanemiller.com
www.edcpub.com

Library of Congress Control Number: 2008933427

Printed and bound in China by Regent Publishing Services, Ltd.
2 3 4 5 6 7 8 9 10

ISBN: 978-1-935279-00-6

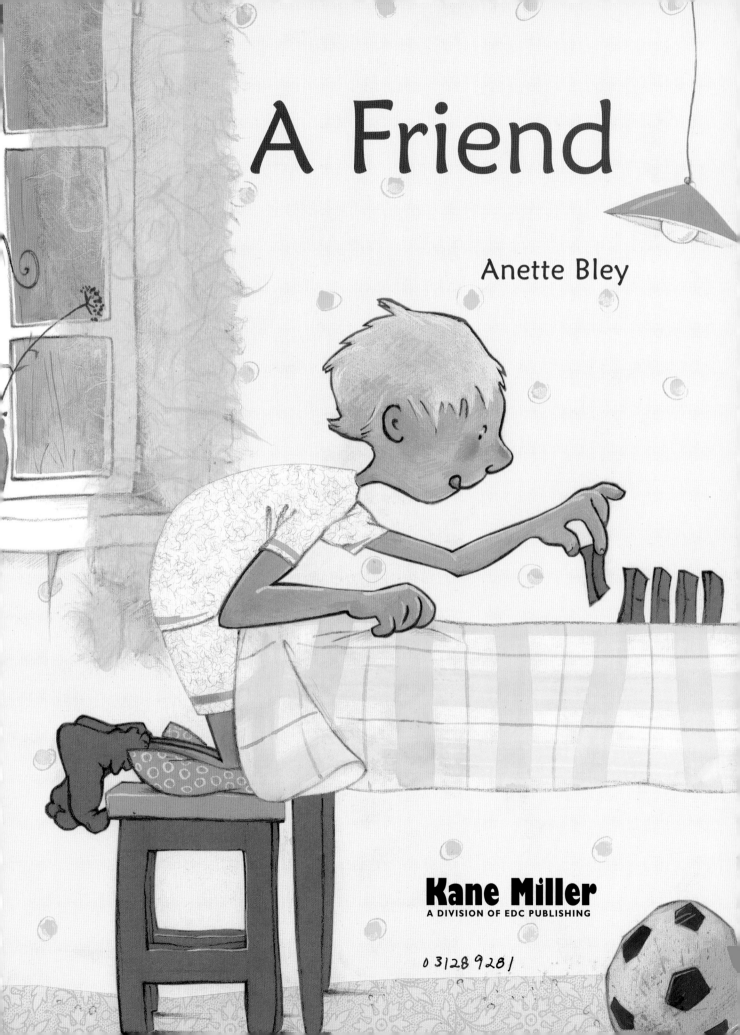

A Friend

Anette Bley

Kane Miller
A DIVISION OF EDC PUBLISHING

0 3128 9281

I'm glad I have a friend to play with ...

Someone to get in trouble with ...

... on rainy days.

... when I feel
like playing tricks.

Someone to
dance and
laugh with ...

... when I am happy.

A friend
who is quiet
with me ...

... when
I am sad.

Someone who
is there …

... whenever I need help.

But who doesn't try to help ...

... when I want to do things on my own.

A friend who has the courage
to tell me the truth ...

... when everyone else is laughing.

Someone who tells me stories ...

... when I need them.

A friend wh
holds me ...

And lets
me go ...

... when I
need to be
comforted.

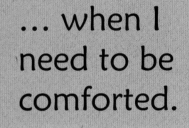

... when I
ask them to.

Someone
who is like
me ...

Someone who is completely
different from me ...

... when everything else is new and strange.

... when I am at peace with myself and the world.

Someone who forgives me for my mistakes ...

Someone who corrects my mistakes ...

... when I feel small
and foolish.

... when I want to   learn.

Someone
I can
trust ...

... when I'm
in trouble.

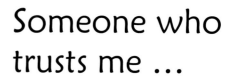

... when no one
else seems to.

Someone who shares with me ...

Someone who shares with me ...

... when I am hungry.

... when I am not.

... when I am far from home.

... when adventure calls.

... when I feel lost.

... when I am ready.

Someone who likes me ...

Someone who believes in me ...

Someone who will take the time to be with me ..

... even when they don't like
the things I do.

... when I dare to try something new.

... doing nothing at all.

Someone who shares
all their secrets.

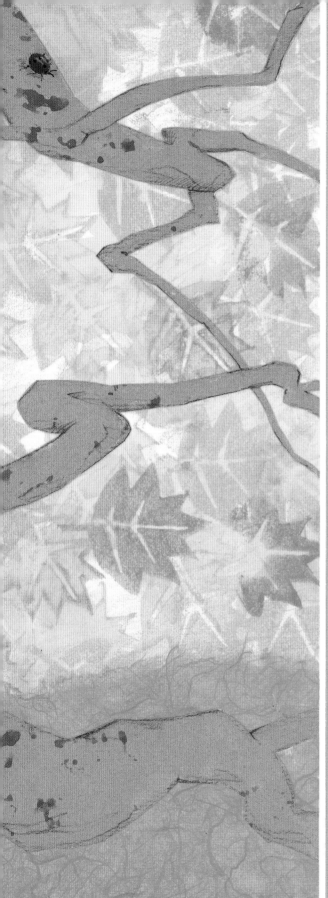

Who is
your friend ...

... when you want
to dance and laugh?

... when everything
is new and strange?

... when you're
in trouble?

Someone who
hears all of mine.

... so I could play too.

I'd like a friend ...

... who'd need me.

... who would listen.

...who would care.

... who sing

... who doesn't fight.

... to hold my hand.

... who wouldn't replace me with someone else, just because.